MIDNIGHT KING

SHIFTER ISLAND BOOK THREE

LEIA STONE

RAYE WAGNER

❀ Created with Vellum

CHAPTER ONE

"I'll be right back," Nai whisper-shouted in my ear, her breath fanning over my neck. She kissed me on the cheek and then followed her grandfather's shield, Reyna, behind the stage.

As my mate stepped away, I followed her with my gaze until the throng of wolf shifters at my coronation swallowed her. *Mother Mage, I love her.*

As if to reinforce the thought, my memory produced an image of her lying beneath me, her head back and eyes heavy-lidded with passion. She parted her kiss-swollen lips and moaned my name. My body instantly responded, and I shoved the image away—for now. There'd be plenty of time tonight to make new memories with her.

I sucked in a ragged breath and turned my attention to the buzzing auditorium.

The shifters' cheers filled my ears, and I grinned

like a lunatic as my gaze roved over the crowd. These people, *my people,* cheered … for *me.*

Noble elbowed me. *'They're waiting for you to announce the celebrations.'*

Crap.

I'd been so wrapped up in Nai that I'd forgotten the task at hand.

"Let the celebration begin," I bellowed over the noise.

The doors at the back of the hall opened, and dozens of serving staff filed in, bringing with them silver-covered platters heaped with hors d'oeuvres, prime rib, desserts, and crates of mage wine. A breath later, the air was filled with the scents of roasted steak, yeast rolls, and cinnamon. My mouth watered, and my stomach growled. That dominance fight had been a bad one even though Nai's blood helped heal me. A good meal would hurry the process along.

"I'm so proud of you, Courage," my mom said when she suddenly appeared, stepping around Noble with a grin. She hugged me tightly and then pulled back to study me closely. "I always knew you'd live up to your name."

"Holy hells," Noble said, shaking his head as he stared at our mom with wide eyes. "We have to live up to our names?"

My mom raised her eyebrows at Noble and wagged her finger in mock chagrin. "Swearing is *not* noble."

I rolled my eyes behind my mom's back, but I

wasn't about to step between them. Justice headed in our direction, weaving out of the crowd, and handed me a plate piled to the top, and his gaze flickered over the crowd nearby.

"Where's Nai?" he asked, holding up another plate, this one piled with a different assortment than my own: chicken, not beef, lots of fruit, and a bowl filled with liquid chocolate.

I nodded at the corner of the room she'd disappeared to while taking a hunk of steak into my mouth. "She said she'd be right back, went off with Reyna. I think her grandfather is sick. He hasn't been looking so well lately."

Justice nodded. "He's been a great help to us, but the old man is getting on in years."

"Long live our alpha king, King Courage!" John bellowed.

More than my name, the title made me freeze. *Alpha king*. Somehow, despite every obstacle we'd faced, Nai and I had made it happen. Together.

Nathan took up the chant as well, followed by the alpha from Harvest.

The cheer built while Nathan, Nai's dad and the alpha of Crescent, bumped into me.

"Come on," Nathan said. His gaze jumped from me to John, the new alpha of Daybreak. "Help me hoist him up. Let the wolves see their king!"

Mom took my plate before I could drop it, and the

next thing I knew, the room was filled with a chorus of "Long live the king!"

I was hoisted into the air on John's and Nathan's shoulders as a grin swept across my face. I'd waited for this moment a long time. My uncle was an asshole on the best of days, and although I respected his seat of power, I'd come to disagree with the way he ran the wolves. This was my chance, my chance to show not just the wolves what kind of king I could be but the other shifters as well.

After a few laps around the room, the guys put me back down on the ground, and the crowd erupted into another round of cheers as each of the pack alphas patted me on the back, offering their congratulations. I felt so proud to be their king, proud to be so warmly accepted by all of them.

Well, *most* of them. When I scanned the crowd, I spotted Mallory and her sister as well as several others from Daybreak as they slipped out the large, front, double door.

Beyond disrespectful, but how could I blame them?

'You're frowning,' Justice growled, poking me.

Mallory and Daybreak's dissenters were a problem for future-Rage. I wanted to enjoy this moment as alpha king.

I forced a smile and waved, and the wolves responded with another round of bellowed applause.

Where was Nai? I wanted my mate to share in this moment with me. Maybe I'd just run back and check on her quickly—no one would even miss me. I stepped toward the stage—

"Speech! Speech! Speech!" the crowd chanted, and I chuckled.

I nodded to my brother. *'Honor, go tell Nai to come out here. She's going to miss my amazing speech.'*

His sleek black fur darted through the crowd and to the back of the room as I cleared my throat and stepped up onto the stage.

"Wolves…" I took a deep breath and reached for my rehearsed words. This was it… "Wolves of Alpha Island." The crowd hushed. "I stand before you now as your alpha king"—cheers erupted once more, and I waited for them to die down before I continued—"I want to thank you, not only for your support but also this opportunity to serve you. While there are many things I could say today, plans I could share for our future … I want you to know my goal is not to rule over you, to invoke fear or repress any of our kind. I want to be a just and loyal king. I believe we are better, stronger, and more powerful *together*. My singular goal as your leader is to bring unity to our packs and for all our kind. Thank you!"

The people cheered wildly.

"Now, let's celebrate to our future!" I raised my fist into the air, and Noble stepped up behind me and slipped a crown on my head.

The wolf shifters howled and cheered, and the din became deafening.

'Now that you're alpha king, you could *tell them all to settle down,'* Noble said into my mind.

As alpha king, I could do a lot more than that. I could speak into any wolf shifter's mind, regardless of whether they were in human form or wolf and regardless of which clan they belonged to. Not only that, my human mind would be present when I was in my wolf form. No more wolf instinct overruling human reason. No more speaking by instinct either.

I grinned at Noble. *'But where's the fun in that?'*

The lights dimmed, and the music started, a deep bass reverberating through the floor. My gaze slid to the empty throne beside me, and I frowned. This moment was *almost* perfect; I only needed my mate at my side.

'Nai?' I called out to her, opening myself to try to sense where she was. We hadn't completed our mate bond yet, but we were close enough that—

Shock wormed through me, followed by sadness and fear. The feelings were not mine, which meant…

What the hell?

I stiffened with understanding and shot Justice a look.

'Find out what's going on with Nai,' I snapped, sending the order to my brother before I'd considered my words, and I tacked on a hasty, *'Please.'*

She hadn't responded, but I felt slightly better watching Justice run out the side door to find her.

It was tempting to reach out to her again, but whatever she was going through had her in an emotional knot, enough so that her anxiety coursed through our unfinished mate bond. I wondered if it had anything to do with her ill grandfather. She was tough. She didn't take shit. But … I had no idea how much she could handle before she broke.

Everyone had a limit, and I wanted to be there if something devastating had happened.

'Where is she?' I asked Honor while wondering how rude it would be if I left my own coronation party to go look for her.

'She's walking with her grandfather into the library,' Honor said.

My chest squeezed, and I forced a deep breath.

'The library? Follow her!' I shot the thought out to Honor and started down the stage steps.

'On it,' Honor replied.

Why was she going to the library in the middle of my coronation party?

Regardless of how I felt or even how Nai felt, I needed to show strength to my people—especially right now. These first few days, and likely weeks, were precarious. I knew it. Hell, I'd trained my entire life for this. I knew every rule and social nicety, what behavior was acceptable, what would be tolerated, and what would earn me the scorn of my new subjects—like me disappearing at my own coronation. But when it came to Nai, I was willing to break all the rules.

I gave the biggest fake smile I could muster as I

attempted to pass through the crowd, but they pushed in on me, wanting to shake my hand or say a few words. I tried to oblige them as quickly as possible, but they kept coming.

'Honor? What is she doing?'

My adrenaline spiked when he didn't immediately answer. Then, Noble stepped in front of me, frowning. I could see the terror I felt reflected in his face.

'Honor!' I clenched my fists, and my heart raced when he didn't immediately respond. Noble began to part the crowd, making me a path to pass through.

The wolves cheered and howled, but now the sound grated against my nerves, leaving me raw.

'She's walking fast. I'm tracking them,' Honor replied.

My panic went full-blown. *'Tracking them?'* I snarled. *'How the hell did they get away from you?'*

He said nothing, and it was only Noble's hands on my shoulders that kept me from losing my mind.

"Rage?" Noble's eyes were wide and panicked, and his voice filled with urgency. My brothers and I had our own bond, and he could likely feel my turmoil. "What's wrong?"

This time, I spoke into all of my brothers' minds. *'Nai was with her grandfather and Reyna. They disappeared into the library. Something's wrong. I feel it.'*

Justice growled in my head before I'd even finished the last word.

'Honor!' My chest heaved with each short breath. The only way she'd just disappear and *not* tell me what

the hell was happening was if she was kidnapped, right?

Would her own grandfather kidnap her? No … he'd done nothing but help her. Then, what was she doing? My mind raced as panic clawed at me. Why wasn't she answering me? Why did she feel so far away? *'Nai!'*

I finally got through the double doors and slammed right into Justice.

As soon as I saw the look on my brother's face, I knew…

"No." My legs went weak as I scanned my best friend's face. White as a sheet, Justice looked on the verge of tears. He, of all people, knew how much Nai meant to me; he knew how much I'd struggled with hiding my fated-mate marks from her—and how much I'd struggled with being fated mates with a member of my pack's sworn enemy.

"She's … gone."

Justice's words sank into me, but everything in me rebelled at his statement.

"What do you mean *gone*?" My wolf surged to the surface. Pelts of fur bristled from my skin, and I clenched my jaw.

Justice frowned. "The guards saw her, Reyna, and Nai's grandfather leave the castle and head toward the school. I picked up her scent. Honor was with them, but his scent is gone now, too."

No.

She wouldn't leave me… "Where did they go? Where does their scent end?"

Justice swallowed, and a pit opened in my stomach that grew wider the longer he delayed.

"The portal door in the library…"

My stomach dropped out as nausea washed over me.

No.

She wouldn't.

There was a high mage portal in the library. But … her grandfather wouldn't take her to High Mage Island, would he?

"Rage…" Justice's voice forced me to look at him. "The guard who saw her said she went … *willingly.*"

No. I didn't believe that. I couldn't.

The party still raged; music from inside filtered throughout the courtyard. The smell of sweat and mage wine pressed against me, and all around, the sounds of joy and laughter and celebration…

She was supposed to be here. Supposed to be by my side. My mate. Nai wouldn't leave.

Not willingly.

"Sound the alarm," I barked to Justice. "Lock down the campus. Post two guards at every boat dock. Send out the scent dogs." He gave me a pitying look. Then, I tore across the open courtyard, headed to the library.

Justice ran after me. *'Brother, she's gone. Honor too. I tracked their scent. You know I'm the best.'*

Unbridled rage, unlike anything I'd ever felt before,

surged up inside of me. *'Lock down those damn borders, Justice! My mate has been kidnapped!'*

'Nai! Where are you?' I pushed the thought into her mind, trying to search for her energy, but…

I couldn't feel her.

'Nai!' I shouted, grasping the sides of my head as I ran.

CHAPTER TWO

MY WOLF SURGED to the surface, and I let him take over. This form was better suited for scenting and was faster. We sprinted across the courtyard, entered the main building through a doggie-door big enough to let our wolf forms through, and then proceeded to the library as we followed Nai's smell.

As my brothers and I approached the library doors, I shifted back to my human form and stared down the two guards posted at the door.

"Did you two let her in here?" I barked even as I wondered how in the hell they'd arrived here. I didn't have anyone posted at the school during my coronation. Alpha Academy was closed.

"Rage," Justice said beside me. "I posted them here five minutes ago."

I shook myself, trying to get a grip on reality.

Reaching out, I grasped the door handle and

shoved. I burst through the library doors so hard they hit the wall with a crack, and the glass insets shattered. Weaving through the aisles toward the back of the room, I ran, and my pulse climbed the closer I got to the black stone door.

It was closed.

On hands and knees, I inhaled, and a whimper ripped through me as Nai's sunshine and homey scent filled my soul. Honor's musky scent was there too.

I climbed to my feet as fury filled every corner of my being. She wouldn't have done this to me.

My entire life, I'd never even tried to open that black stone door; the rules stated we weren't allowed.

But today, I was king, so screw the rules. I was going after my mate.

I launched myself forward with an angry cry on my lips.

"No!" Justice shouted.

No sooner had my palm touched the Onyx surface than a searing blue light shot from the door. My fingers burned with pain. A yip left my throat, and my body arched. An electric charge filled the space, and I was thrown back by protective magic, crashing into a shelf of books, toppling it over. The smell of my burning skin filled the air.

"Rage!" Justice ran to me. When he reached down to pull me up, the pity in his expression made my entire body heavy with dread. I couldn't follow her.

This isn't happening...

My mate left me at my own coronation?

He must have spelled her. Her grandfather was helpful with getting Honor back, but who knew his real intentions? That had to be it.

With a heave, Justice got me into a standing position, but I just stood there, swaying as my mind raced through every horrible scenario possible.

"Cursed council," Noble huffed, appearing at my side sniffing the air like a dog. "What did you do?"

I shot him a glare and raised my blackened, still-smoking palm, gritting my teeth to keep from screaming. He doused my hand with his water magic as the agony traveled up my arm and spotted my vision.

With a howl of frustration, I shifted back into my wolf-form and sniffed. Sure enough, not only was Nai's scent all of the way to the edge of the black stone door, Honor's, Reyna's, and that damned High Mage Master of Spirit's smell was there too. They all left. Together. Without me.

What a shady bastard!

I morphed back into my human form, grabbed the nearest wooden chair, and hurled it at the stone door.

"How dare you!" I bellowed. Fresh pain coursed up my arm, but it was nothing compared to the anguish in my soul. *Betrayal.* Either by Geoff or Nai or both. And certainly by Honor.

Justice cleared his throat. "Maybe—"

I reeled on him and snarled, "Don't you dare defend her. Or him. Or any of them. Don't. You.

Dare." I heaved a breath and pivoted. "Noble," I barked at my more sensible brother. "I need to send a letter to the High Mage Council," I growled. "If they do not return my mate immediately, I will start a war."

Noble blanched. "Brother, wait a second. What if Nai *did* go willingly as Justice said and—"

"She wouldn't do that to me," I growled. Didn't they know of our love? No. That wasn't even a possibility.

Justice just gave me a sympathetic look that made me want to bludgeon something—or someone—anyone really.

"If she did," Noble continued, "I'd advise you not to out her to the rest of the High Mage Council. If they're not in on it, you could get her into trouble."

Crap. He had a point.

Without looking at Justice or Noble, I returned to the door and the guards.

I kept my attention on the men, both from our pack and around our same age, but the one on the left was a year younger than us. "Richie," I snarled, my voice still barely human. "Has anyone gone in or out since Justice put you here?"

The dark-haired guard shook his head. "No, sir. I mean, not besides you guys. The high mages came by—"

My blood boiled. "When?"

Richie swallowed. "Maybe a minute before you did. They said they wanted to use the portal to go home—"

My nostrils flared, and I struggled to keep my wolf in check. "And?"

"I … I told them we had orders from the alpha king that no one could go in." He winced. "So they left. One of them said they'd use the other portal. Sorry, I hope that was the right thing to do. I overheard Prince Justice speaking about Nai—Queen Nai—disappearing, and I figured you would want to lock down the exits…" He dropped his chin to his chest.

I clapped a hard hand on his shoulder. "You did good."

I wasn't going to be an a-hole on my first day as king just because I was in a crisis. Besides, he might've just bought us time to catch up with them.

My thoughts jumped to the secluded area on Daybreak's lands where the high mages could enter and exit our island, and I whispered to myself, "Other portal."

"Noble." I turned to my brother and ignored his wide, panicked expression. "I'm putting you in charge."

"But—"

"No," I growled, clenching my fists. "You're the only one I trust to run things while we're gone. If Justice and I aren't back in an hour, send a letter through the official channels to the High Mage Council, requesting that *my mate* be returned. Promptly."

Noble gulped but nodded his head.

Turning my attention to Justice, I took in his dark, murderous expression, mirroring my exact mood. He was usually the more reserved and stoic of us. He was my ride or die, loyal to me in *everything*. I didn't even have to ask; he just nodded.

"Lead the way, bro," he said, the words clipped and short, and waved for me to move ahead. As I passed him, he whispered, "We'll get her back."

Emotion wrung my chest and clogged my throat.

I knew he was right. I was being an irrational fool, but Nai wasn't just my girlfriend or my mate. We were *fated* mates; she was the other half of my soul. Something horrific had to be going on for her to leave me—especially like this.

First, find Nai. Then, fix whatever *it* was that made her leave. No matter the cost.

My skin turned to fur, muscles bulking and tendons snapping over my cracking bones as I shifted to my wolf.

The other portal to High Mage Island—maybe there were more, but these two were the only ones I knew of—lay on the other side of the island, on *Daybreak* lands.

'I'm sending five guards with you and Justice,' Noble pressed into my mind. *'You're king now. You need proper security.'*

'Fine.' Whatever. I didn't care about protocol, security, or even my crown. My fated mate was missing, and she was the only thing I could think about right now.

JUSTICE AND I RAN—FASTER and harder than ever before. The silence between us was heavy and taut, my emotions roiling through me as the darkened forest blurred past. I processed my anger at the situation, trying to make sense of it—any of it.

The trees thinned, opening into a large glade in front of us. Waves crashed below a rocky overhang. Daybreak's lands butted up against the north shore of the island. Dense forest and rocky cliffs mixed with the salty air of the sea. Trails to the beach wound through the terrain, but this was the best place on Alpha Island for cliff diving and rock climbing.

My uncle had brought me here once each year since my twelfth birthday to show me the high mage portal and discuss battle strategies. If we were to ever be attacked, Declan always said it would come from our north side.

His voice echoed in my mind, and I cringed at how much I had wanted to be like him. I'd seen him as cold and distant but a strong, calculating leader—not for the psychotic maniac he was.

'Nai?' I tried her for the umpteenth time. The only other couple I had ever heard of being fated mates from two different worlds were Nai's deceased parents. So I had no idea of what we were capable of. Hell, I wasn't sure if anyone did. Not that it mattered; I wouldn't give up.

'Was John still at the coronation party?' I asked Noble, inquiring about the new alpha of Daybreak.

I'd killed the former alpha of Daybreak, Mallory's dad, and traipsing onto John's land without seeking his consent was disrespectful, but he'd understand, right? I was king, and this was Nai ... I needed her back—now. He and Sara had been so nice to Nai and me when we were on his land before. I didn't think he'd mind now.

'I think so,' Noble said and then confirmed it a breath later.

Justice slowed his pace as his nostrils flared. Then, he bared his teeth. *'Mallory here.'*

I'd already picked up on her scent, but I hoped she'd take off rather than confront us.

The five guards Noble sent trotted up behind us, huffing and puffing. Apparently, the entire royal guard needed to increase their training and conditioning. Declan had become overconfident and lax. I wasn't stupid. A new king would always be tested—even if I didn't know how or when. I'd need a strong guard to protect our borders and a group of trusted elites to help keep my loved ones safe.

'They're close,' I shot back to Justice. A breeze carried their scent nearer, and I sniffed the ground, trying to pinpoint their location. *'As in right around—'*

"What the hell are you doing here, Rage?" Mallory growled, stepping out from the trees behind me.

Her sister followed her, muttering, "Come to rub salt in our wounds?"

I spun, shifting into my human form with extra caution to use magic and keep my clothing on. Mallory had tried to hook up with me my second year at Alpha Academy, and she'd been a bitch to Nai. The last thing I wanted was to be naked in front of her.

"Or are you here to finish off the rest of our family?" Mallory spat.

"I'm not here to kill you," I huffed, rolling my eyes. I didn't know what else to say to her without sounding like a dick. *I'm sorry for your loss, but your dad was a prick and deserved it?*

She stepped closer, her eyes glistening with unshed tears, and her body trembled.

Next to me, Justice, already back in his human form, snorted with derision. Even before Nai, he'd hated Mallory.

My guards stalked closer, still in their wolf forms, as Mallory stepped into my personal space.

"You could have let him live!" Her scream cut off as a sob ripped from her throat.

I sighed. There was no joy for me in her pain, but she was wrong. I couldn't have let him live.

"Alpha fights end only with death. You know this, and so did he," I said.

She glared at me. "Then, why are you here?" she growled through clenched teeth, stepping closer.

Justice stepped forward, chin held high, and gently pushed her back. "Have some respect for *your king*."

Mallory balked, eyes widening, and then she lowered her gaze and her chin while I flicked a gaze to my brother.

'She's grieving. Let it go…' I almost said before I remembered how Mallory and her siblings had joined Nolan in trying to kill my mate during the mid-year games. As king, I'd need to deal with that kind of behavior. Might as well set the standard now.

I stepped up to her, toe-to-toe, and stared her down, letting all of my anger and frustration surge to the surface. "I don't need permission to go anywhere on Alpha Island. I'm *king*," I told her, my voice barely human. "And this is your official notice that you've both been expelled from Alpha Academy for unsportsmanlike conduct." I looked to her sister to make sure she knew I was talking about her as well. "If you ever attack my mate or my family, I'll personally watch my guards tear you to shreds. Don't challenge me again, Mallory Daybreak."

Then, I blasted past her and her sister, not noticing the four other Daybreak wolves who'd left my coronation early with the girls until afterward. I ignored them all; I didn't want them to think I was a pushover. Best to be stern now and not have to deal with another challenge fight later, but I was glad Noble had the foresight to send extra guards. Not that these six would be a challenge, but a fight would take time.

As for Mallory and her sister's expulsion, it was the best way to limit her training and decrease the potential that she or her sister challenge John in the future for alpha of their pack. Besides, with John as alpha, his daughters had a rightful spot at Alpha Academy as his heirs.

A low whine of submission came from Mallory's throat as I passed, but she didn't move from her place by the tall cedar tree. Good riddance.

Once Justice and I entered the clearing, I scanned the land.

Several homes sat near the edge of the cliff, overlooking the water; the rest of the pack's homes were scattered throughout the territory. I glanced at the castle-like monstrosity Mallory had been raised in. Her father had been just like Declan, cold and calculating.

Dismissing her and her father from my thoughts, I scanned the trees on the northernmost tip of the clearing. As soon as I found the tree, I'd find the portal. Once I found the portal, I'd hopefully find my mate.

My heart thundered with eager anticipation as my thoughts narrowed until my sole focus was Nai. I walked to the right, along the cliff, until I reached the copse. Then, weaving through the trees, I searched for the weeping willow among the juniper, pines, cedars, and firs.

High Mage Island overlaid Alpha Island, but the former resided in another dimension we couldn't see or access. They were protected in their elite plane of existence, and as far as I knew, there were only two portals in or out: the library and the weeping willow.

I stepped between two giant cedar trunks, feeling the scrub and undergrowth brushing against my legs, and then pulled to a stop. There it was, a curly willow tree sitting in a much smaller clearing of grass. The tree's naked limbs looked sorely out of place, turning orange in the fading sunlight. Between the bare branches, the light caught on a shimmering kaleidoscope of colors.

"This is it?" Justice walked up beside me. "The tree?"

I nodded while considering the best approach. "There's no door. No lock." I took a deep breath, hoping it would be easy. "Maybe we just walk through like the portal to the mortal world."

"Maybe." Justice rubbed the back of his neck and narrowed his eyes at the intricately woven branches. Finally, he turned his attention to me. "I'll try it first."

"I'm king, not made of glass." I rolled my eyes and stepped forward.

My brother grabbed my arm and pulled me back. "I wasn't implying you were made of glass, idiot, but if this thing shreds you to pieces, I'll be king. Neither of us wants that."

"Good point." I glanced down at my hand, noting the charred skin already flaking away and showing hints of pink, new skin underneath. High mage magic was potent stuff. I carried a hefty amount of elemental fire magic, but it was nothing like the power used in making these portals.

"I'm not sure I want you walking through either," I said to Justice, holding up my healing hand.

Footsteps announced several visitors, and my lip curled when I caught Mallory's scent.

"They've spelled them with protections," she said, "so only high mages are able to use them. You can't get through without breaking the spells."

"How would you know that?" I asked, facing her with a glare. "And why would I trust you?"

I then looked at one of my five guards. Could I ask one of them to risk their life like this? "Oh, screw this."

I wanted my damn mate, and I wanted her *now*! This was *my* fight for her, so I'd get her.

Sucking in a deep breath, I parted the long stringy branches and stepped toward the shimmering light—only to have Justice pull me back. Again. As I spun on my heel, a black tennis shoe hurtled past my face and hit the colorful wall of magic. With a sharp, loud zap, the shoe disappeared, leaving a puff of dark smoke and the acrid stench of burning rubber in the air.

Shit.

Maybe this was a time to think more and act less. That could've been bad. I shook my head, trying to dislodge the panicked, desperate thoughts driving me. Being without Nai, thinking she was hurt, was tearing me up inside, but I wanted us together *alive*.

"You owe me new sneakers." Justice patted my shoulder, but his demand fell empty and discarded.

All I saw was the pity in his eyes.

My attention flicked to my guards, and I balled my fists. "Jonas and Garret, fetch the master mages from school: Carn, Jin, and Helo. We'll have them break the protection spells." I faced Justice and growled with frustration. "I don't care about the repercussions."

The two guards raced off, back toward the school, and I resisted the urge to follow.

'Just tell Noble to send the mages up here,' Justice spoke into my mind. *'You'll cut down on travel time that way.'*

I rested my hand on Justice's shoulder. I wasn't thinking clearly; everything was a panic in my mind. *'Thank you.'*

I repeated the request to Noble, who assured me he'd get right on it.

'Stay there until I know something,' Noble said. *'No sense in you running around the island like a chicken with your head cut off.'*

But I couldn't just stand here, waiting. I paced the small glen, pausing at each end to glance at the tree. The more I looked at the damn tree, the more I debated another trial like with the door in the library.

'Don't do it,' Justice said, making me jump.

I met his gaze, and he shook his head.

'I know you want her back. We all do,' he said. *'We'll get her back, bro. But she'll skin you alive if you do anything stupid.'*

'How do you know I was going to do anything stupid?' I snapped, my frustration boiling over.

He snorted. *'You've got stupid written all over your face.'*

A heavy, sinking feeling pulled through my chest and then churned through my gut.

'*Rage?*' Noble's voice, filled with trepidation, hit me, like a punch to my stomach. '*The master mages are gone. You gave them the weekend off, remember?*'

'*Gone,*' I repeated stupidly, and my gaze jerked to Justice. '*Why did I let them leave? Stupid.*'

Justice gave me a pitying look, but it was Noble who answered.

'*There's a meeting on the High Mage Island. They said it was to discuss the best approach to a relationship with a new king. I totally forgot until now. I'm sorry, bro.*'

Panic coursed through me, and each breath tore at my chest. I swallowed hard and looked to Justice.

'*I'm out of ideas, brother. What if she's hurt? What if she needs help and I can't get to her? What if her grandfather was bad this whole time and he's hurting her—?*'

'*No.*' Justice growled. '*We can't think like that. Come on, I've got an idea.*'

When he turned and started to shift into his wolf form, I followed him, ignoring Mallory and her little crew, who were likely glaring daggers at my back. I needed my mate.

'*Nai! Where are you?!*'

CHAPTER THREE

"THIS IS BRILLIANT," I told Justice as we drove through the streets of Mageville towards the portal that led from the Magic Lands to the mortal realm in Montana. There was *always* a high mage or advanced level mage working the portal. I could ask—no, *demand* they let me through one of the portals on Alpha Island. Or at least demand they return my mate to me. "Why didn't I think of it?" I mused under my breath.

Justice cast me a side-eyed look from the passenger seat. "Panic turns your brain to mush."

"I only panic when it relates to Nai," I admitted, thinking about all the stupid decisions I'd made when I discovered she was my fated mate. "One day, you'll find your mate and know what it's like." I chuckled, thinking of my stoic brother chasing after a girl. "I can't wait to see how you roll when you're in love."

He just shook his head and pointed to the road.

"If you scare one more mage, I'm going to take over as driver," he said, referring to the cloaked figure walking in the ditch rather than the sidewalk because of my distracted, high-speed driving.

Fair enough.

My mouth dried as we exited the populated parts of Mageville and headed toward the dense woods at the border. I just hoped Kian wasn't on duty. That asshole wasn't someone I wanted to owe a favor—let alone ask one of him.

As we approached the border, Nai's aunt stepped into view, and I sagged into my seat with relief. Of all the mages I could have found here, she was the only one I was inclined to trust. She'd helped us once; surely, she'd help again—especially because Nai's safety was something we both wanted.

I pulled over to the side of the road and put the car in park. Rolling down the window of our SUV, I was relieved to see that when she saw me, she smiled. Genuinely.

No hate there.

"Greetings, King Courage of Midnight," she said, her voice like wind chimes.

News traveled fast.

I returned her smile. "Greetings, Sariah. I'm so glad to see you. I need a favor, and it's kind of urgent." This was no time to shoot the shit and ask about the weather. I wanted Nai in my arms. I needed to inspect every inch of her for injuries and then take her to bed. "I hope you can help."

She frowned and tilted her head, her eyebrows pulling down exactly like Nai's did when she was inspecting something. Crazy how much she looked like Nai.

"What's wrong?" Sariah asked, dropping her voice and leaning forward.

My voice shook a little. "Nai's gone. I'm not sure if she was kidnapped or—"

"Kidnapped!" Her eyes went wide.

I nodded. "She was with her grandfather, and then they left to High Mage Island—in the middle of my coronation. She wouldn't take off and not tell me *anything*—"

"Oooh." Sariah drew back as understanding dawned on her face. She offered me a small smile filled with pity. "I see."

'What the hell does that mean?' Justice asked through our bond, his voice barely human as he growled.

I didn't bother answering because I didn't know. Instead, I clenched the steering wheel and leaned out the window, trying to keep my smile in place when all I wanted to do was bellow in frustration.

"You see *what?*" I ground my teeth and tried again. "What exactly do you see? Do you know where she is? Because if you know, I need you to open a portal to my mate. Right *now.*"

She winced, drawing back from me. "I'm sorry, but

... I *can't*. I'm not powerful enough to open the High Mage Island portals, only this one leading to the human world. I'm half-human." She gestured to the portal in front of us as if that would make any sense to me. What did being half-human have to do with anything? But maybe it mattered in the world of magic.

Fur rippled down my arms as I cursed and punched the steering wheel. From the corner of my eye, I noticed she took another step backward.

'Rein it in, Rage,' Justice snapped. *'You're scaring her.'*

"I'm sorry." I forced a deep breath. Justice was right. I needed Sariah right now, and she'd been nothing but nice. I didn't want to scare her. Even if she couldn't open a portal to Nai, the mage in front of me could still help. "Do you know why Nai would go with your father to High Mage Island?"

She grimaced. "I do ... but I can't tell you."

Grinding my teeth together, I looked at Justice, and it took every ounce of self-control I had not to shift.

"*Can't* or *won't*?" I asked, my voice sharp enough to cut glass.

"Can't," she insisted, relaxing enough to offer me a small smile. "Just as you're spelled not to talk about Alpha Academy, I'm spelled about what happens at High Mage Academy. I'm *truly* sorry."

Wait. She said High Mage Academy, not High Mage Island. Why would Sariah say that? Was it a clue? I tried to read her gaze, but it was just patient and kind. "Is Nai ... entering High Mage Academy?"

Sariah shrugged. "I don't know."

Narrowing my eyes, I sucked in a deep breath. "You—"

"I've told you all I can," she said, her expression twisting with regret. "I'm sorry."

My heart turned to stone and then sank into my stomach. "Can you...?" I cleared my throat. "Do you know if she's safe?"

I stared at her, watching her reaction, trying to convey how much I needed this answer.

The rest of the tension fled her body, and her smile returned. "If she's with my father, she's the safest she can be in the High Mage Realm. He loves her very much, and he'd never let *anything* happen to her." Her smile faltered, and then she added, "Not if he can help it ... while he's still alive."

Okay...

I processed what she said, zeroing in on her last comments because both were wholly *not* reassuring. New questions raced through my mind. Was Sariah implying Grampa Geoff was ... *dying*? And if so, was that enough reason for Nai to leave in the middle of my freaking coronation? Did they go for some healing serum? And what did that have to do with High Mage Academy? I had more questions than answers—

'Rage!' Noble's voice cut through my racing thoughts. *'Get back here pronto, dude. We've got a problem.'*

Dammit!

Why did crap always happen in threes? Hadn't we already had enough?

My attention jumped back to Sariah. "If I give you a note, can you get it to Nai? Please?"

She nodded. "Of course. I'll take it to her as soon as I'm able."

'Rage!' Noble yelled again as I leaned over Justice to rummage through the glovebox.

'I'll be there as soon as I can,' I shot back, my frustration mounting as I pulled out gum wrappers and empty mint tins.

Justice pushed me back with one hand and held a pen out to me with the other.

'This is important,' Noble snapped, his tone sharp with fear. *'A bunch of lower mages are here—'*

Lower mages weren't *my* problem.

'This is more important!' I growled, grinding my teeth together when I considered my abysmal options for a note to my mate: crumpled gum wrapper or Nai's aunt's hand.

"If you want me to just pass along a message..." Sariah said, resting her fingers on my arm. "I'll remember it word for word, I promise."

I nodded and nudged the car back into drive.

"Will you please tell her..." I thought of all the things I wanted to say, but really, all my thoughts boiled down to two sentences. "Tell her I love her, and ... please, *please,* come home to me."

"I'll make sure she gets the message," Sariah said.

As soon as I'd murmured my appreciation, I glanced at Justice and jerked my head back toward the island. "Noble's in a panic," I muttered to Justice. "Something with a group of lower mages."

After bidding Sariah goodbye, I spun the car around and raced back through the deepening night to the boat docks at top speed.

A CACOPHONY of revelry still thundered from the coronation party in the auditorium, but Justice and I avoided the melee and headed straight to the conference room where Noble told me he'd be. We walked down the stone hallway, approaching the heavy oak door. Two guards stood outside in the passageway, each with a mace and broadsword, their presence a foreboding omen for what lay within.

I'd been present for a few meetings over the last couple of years with Declan, but never in charge. It was time for me to step up to the plate. When Justice slowed his pace as if he weren't going to attend, I placed a hand on his shoulder, *'Come inside. I may need your help.'*

I surveyed the two guards. Both were at least two decades my senior, old enough to be my father. Noises came from behind the thick wood and stone barriers, voices raised in consternation, but the words were muffled and indistinct.

"What's going on?" I asked, as much to feel the guards out as the situation. On our way back to the castle, I'd reached out to Noble, but he'd been so occupied, dealing with whatever was happening behind these doors, our conversation had been clipped short.

The man on the right, Tad, shook his head. "Your brother, Noble—"

"Prince Noble," Justice growled, correcting the slight.

The guard's lip twitched and then curled in a sneer. "Yes, *Prince* Noble is inside with a bunch of mages from Dark Row."

I frowned. From Dark Row? What the heck were they doing on Alpha Island? Why would mages be *here* asking for help? Unless...

After a nod to Tad, he opened the door, and I strode in, Justice on my heels.

Nearly a dozen lower-level mages, identified by the mage marks on their foreheads, stood around the table, their robes stained with soot and ash. The stench of sweat, blood, and char hung in the air so thick I could taste it at the back of my tongue. The crowd bickered, tones sharp and heated.

"We clearly can't trust the high mages anymore. They don't care about us!" a young, brunette, female mage snapped at a bald mage near her.

We can agree on that, I thought as I zeroed in on the speaker and paused, waiting to hear more.

The bald man glared at the young woman as he

shouted, "So you've said, Beryl, but we don't have enough power without them—"

"The High Mage Council promised us protection!" another male mage bellowed.

"It isn't safe there anymore!" a female screamed.

And the first one, the brunette female mage, raised her voice and screeched over them all. "The high mages are all selfish liars!"

'Good luck, bro,' Justice said in my mind as he went to stand in a corner of the room.

"Mages!" I bellowed, kicking the door shut behind me. It closed with a loud boom, and the room quieted.

Striding into the group, I wound my way through the lower mages until I faced the woman who'd called the high mages liars. I offered her a tight smile and asked, "What can I do for you?"

The young woman was close to our age, within a few years. Her dark hair had been pulled back into a braid that was coming loose, and dark wisps framed her pale skin. She raised her chin and narrowed her blue eyes at me.

"Where are your guards?" she snapped.

I frowned, taken aback by her question and her attitude. I thought the enemy was the high mages, not me. "Here. At the castle, where they should be." I scanned the crowd and found Noble, sighing with relief as he stepped to my side. I faced the young mage once more. "Why do you ask?"

"I told you the new king would be a selfish prick," a woman muttered from my left.

I flinched, trying to control my anger. Nai's sudden disappearance was wearing on my patience.

I kept my attention on the young woman, noting how her jaw hardened, and she balled her hands.

"Your wolves burned down our market, killed and injured dozens of mages, and then you withdraw your guards? If you leave us unprotected, it will be *our* blood on your hands."

Uh ... okay. I hadn't thought about that when I'd pulled the guards from Dark Row, but why would we put guards in Mageville anyway? That wasn't our land to police. And Dark Row burning down had been an accident ... sort of.

I met Justice's gaze from across the room, and his cheeks reddened.

'Sorry, bro.'

'It's fine,' I told him.

"Don't your people have magic? Can't you all just use magic to protect yourselves?" Justice asked from his corner.

I nodded; he was saying exactly what I thought.

"Do you think any advanced mages live in Dark Row, boy? How stupid are you? Our magic isn't strong enough for those kinds of things." She glared at him. "Besides, we need to use what little magic we have to repair what your kind did—by burning Dark Row to the *ground*."

A twinge of guilt wiggled in my chest, and my gaze flicked to Justice, whose embarrassment deepened. I wasn't going to let him take the fall for it though. Really, it was Declan's fault.

"The fire was an accident, and if you'd show me some respect, you'll see I'm *not* a selfish prick." I glared at the woman who'd called me such. "I'll send a dozen guards to help, but only for one week. Mage problems aren't my problems. You have the High Mage Council you can petition for help. You know, your *own kind*."

The dark-haired woman nodded, but the frown pulling at her lips was disconcerting. "Some help they are in their fancy hidden realm. They won't return our communications."

My first day as king, and *nothing* was going to plan.

CHAPTER FOUR

"YOU NEED TO GET SOME SLEEP." Noble's voice shook me from my reverie. I sat in a sleek leather chair behind an ornate mahogany desk, staring at the golden yellow wall in my uncle's office—*my* office now. I skimmed over the four wooden chairs sitting against the back wall to the open door where my brother stood. This place held a lot of bad memories for me. Every time we got into trouble, we were brought here. Usually for a stern word or a beating.

"Honor's with her. That's good," I said, ignoring his comment. I glanced at the clock hanging over the chairs and wondered if Nai's aunt had delivered my message yet.

Noble cleared his throat and, when I looked at him, frowned. "Honor won't let anything happen to her. You've done all you can. Getting some rest will help you to be ready to take on whatever tomorrow brings."

How could I explain that going to bed without her felt like defeat?

"No," I growled and then immediately regretted it. My brother was only trying to help. Justice was now at Dark Row, trying to find any mages powerful enough to break the portal protection spells that kept shifters out of the High Mage Realm, and Noble was here, by my side as usual.

I stood and scooted around the desk, choosing to lean against it rather than take my uncle's fancy seat. I also ignored the overstuffed chairs in front of the fireplace. Everything about this place felt like wearing someone else's suit.

"How is it that we can't go into their world, but they're able to come and go here as they please?" There was more than just a hierarchy of power, and I was starting to see the imbalance more clearly now that I was king.

Noble nodded and crossed the room. "The high mages have always had their secrecy and protection."

He said only what we all knew to be true, but I scoffed at their privilege. "While I'm lending *my* men to guard the nefarious Dark Row?"

Noble shrugged. "That's the Dark Row our brother burned to the ground."

"Technicality," I said, keeping my tone light, and Noble smiled.

"I trust Nai," Noble said. "I also trust her grandfather. He went to the Realm of the Dead to save *you* and *her*. He brought Honor back to life. He wouldn't turn on us now."

He was right, but what did that mean? I ground my teeth in frustration and then asked, "What are you saying? You think we should just wait for her to come back? Don't *do* anything more?"

Noble sighed, dropping his chin, and his black hair fell forward, the dark color highlighting the bags under his eyes. *Shit*. He was probably waiting until I went to sleep before he did. Guilt wormed in my gut because the last few days had been hell for Noble too.

"You can't do anything more, Rage." Noble met my gaze and shook his head. "And if you don't take care of yourself, you're going to start making bad decisions."

I snorted, but there was no sense in arguing.

"We trust Nai, *and* we trust her grandfather, so then maybe they had a good reason for leaving like they did. Maybe she's safe, and you'll hear from her tomorrow."

I narrowed my eyes. "Maybe—"

"I'm not saying, 'Give up.' I'm saying, 'Trust her, and take care of yourself.'"

He was right. I did trust Nai. I trusted her feelings for me and her feelings about us. She was my fated mate; she wouldn't leave me without good reason. The old man was looking beyond ill lately—like death warmed over. Maybe she went to help heal him? Something only she could do like make the healing elixir? Maybe the old man's blood was getting too old to make it himself, and that's why he needed Nai! If he'd started having a heart attack or something, then Nai would've rushed out in a panic, without telling me. I perked up at the thought.

"Okay. Let's get some sleep, and then, tomorrow morning, if she hasn't shown, I'll send a letter to the High Mage Council."

Noble winced. "Let's talk about next steps in the morning."

I growled.

Noble rushed on. "She could be there *in secret.* The High Mage Council doesn't like her as it is."

I wanted to growl again, but this time, my frustration was with the mages, not my brother, so I swallowed it. "Fine."

Noble walked over and placed a hand on each of my shoulders. "For what it's worth, I believe Nai will be back, and ... you'll make a fine king."

Emotion clogged my throat, and for some reason, I thought of our father and how proud he'd be to see me leading with my brothers' support.

I forced a swallow. "Thank you for being here for me."

He smiled and squeezed my shoulders before turning to leave.

When he reached the door, I called out. "Noble?"

Turning to glance over his shoulder, he raised his eyebrows at me, and I gestured to all the stuff in the office. "I want this redecorated, and I'm putting you in charge. Make it nice—and get rid of everything that was Declan's."

A slow grin worked up his mouth and he nodded. "Yes, My King."

After he left the room, my gaze fell to the space in front of the fireplace. A memory surfaced from our childhood—one I always tried to push away—but I let it come this time. My brothers and I were eight years old, and we'd convinced our nanny at the time, a large bear shifter named Nanny Bess, to take us to the market in Mageville to buy our mother a birthday present—a memory glass so she could see memories of our father because we'd all caught her crying about him at one time or another.

I closed my eyes and let the scene play out in my mind's eye.

Nanny Bess ushered us onto a ferry, and we scampered around her, all giddy with excitement. The ride across to the mage lands was filled with laughter, all four of us boys spending the hour-long ferry ride racing up and down the deck and playing hide and seek. As we pulled into the dock, we ran to Nanny Bess and clung to her thick purple skirt. An indentured servant, who probably should've hated us, Nanny Bess treated us with warmth and kindness.

After we disembarked, I stared at the mages as unease twisted my insides. They intimidated me with their strange mage marks and scowling eyes.

But Nanny Bess was bigger and stronger, and she moved with quiet confidence. Soon enough, I forgot all about the smaller-built mages and their scary magic; my attention became riveted on the food. Nanny Bess bought us each a sticky sweet roll, which we ate on our way to the stall where magical artifacts were sold.

In my uncle's office, I shook my head, remembering my own infatuation with the stunning dark mage who'd sold us the memory glass.

Surlama.

As we waited for the ferry back home, a group of bear shifters approached us, and the big male embraced Nanny Bess. One of them, a young girl a few years older than us, broke away from the others and confronted me and my brothers.

"When will your father let my mom go?" she asked, tears in her eyes. "It's not fair to keep her—"

"Hush, Marji," Nanny Bess said, stepping between us and the girl. With her back to us, our nanny kissed the girl's head as the ferry pulled up to the dock. As Justice, Noble, Honor, and I all stared at one another in confusion, our nanny waved at the group of shifters and said, "I'll see you tomorrow."

Just as it had then, my stomach opened to a dark, fathomless pit.

'Those people are her family,' Honor said.

We all knew it.

'Why is she with us and not them?' Justice asked.

I shrugged, just as perplexed as my siblings. We were still young enough that we didn't really understand that Nanny Bess was a hostage and our uncle was her captor.

'You should ask,' Justice said to me, his green eyes wide with worry. 'You're the one with courage.'

So I did—as soon as we were on the boat, I asked Nanny Bess.

"Before you were born, when your father was alpha king, all the shifters lived on the island together," Nanny Bess said.

I stared at her in awe. "All of them?"

She nodded. "But after your father was killed—"

"By those Crescent scum," I snarled, repeating what we'd heard from Declan, so eager to fill in this fact and show my brothers and my nanny that I was smart and on top of things.

Instead of nodding, Nanny Bess pursed her lips and then took a deep breath. "King Declan said the other shifters were inferior to the wolves and were taking up too much of his territory. We needed to leave. When we protested being kicked off the island, the wolves came into our territory and removed us by force."

Her declaration had shocked me and my brothers, and we stared at her, slack-jawed.

"Now, I owe a ten-year penance to the alpha king."

Her statement gutted me then.

'That's not right,' Justice said.

"We'll make Uncle Declan let you go," Honor told her, hugging her waist. "You should be with your family."

I agreed...

But Declan didn't.

Later that night, when I'd asked him to let Nanny Bess

go, he'd slapped me across the face and called me stupid and naïve.

He'd said my brothers and I had let ourselves be manipulated. We were too soft, too loving. Too gullible. We'd trusted a traitor—

And then, when Honor yelled at him to let Nanny Bess go as well...

Declan flew into a rage and hit us all.

With every strike, he admonished us to be wiser, stronger, tougher.

"You are the oldest and the strongest," he'd said, looking down his nose at me. His expression was stern, his voice filled with disappointment. "And therefore, whether you want it or not, you are the alpha of your sibling pack. It is your responsibility, Courage, to make sure nothing like this happens to your family again. You let a traitor worm her way into your heart and steal your common sense. Just look at what that cost your brothers." He waved at Justice, Noble, and Honor, all three of them holding their red cheeks. "If you can't lead a group of four, how will you ever lead a pack of hundreds or thousands? It is time for you to grow up, young man. Lead with your head, not your bleeding heart."

For years, I thought Declan was right.

I toughened myself, closed myself off to anyone or anything that could make me weak. I accepted Declan's abusive words as truth. Even when I went with my brothers to fetch Nai from Montana.

The moment I laid eyes on her in those ripped jeans shorts and tank-top, standing barefoot on her land in

Montana, my wolf had seized up inside of my body. When her scent had hit me, the drive to touch her, taste her, possess her nearly overwhelmed me. I knew then she'd be my ruin if I let her.

So I decided to never let her in.

And then, on the car ride to the portal, she clamped her hand over my mouth. Without even thinking, I'd tasted her skin. A small lick of her finger was all it took, and suddenly, I needed more. But every time I felt desire for Nai, I reminded myself of how weak it would make me. How thinking with my heart had gotten my brothers and me hurt.

Then came the masquerade party…

Hidden behind a mask, I thought a blind hook-up would be enough to satiate my growing desire for Nai, help me walk away from her.

But of all of the masked ladies at the party, I'd been pulled to her—like a magnet. Her kiss was sunshine lighting up the darkest abyss inside of me. It was water in the desert, sustenance to my starving soul. As soon as I kissed her, tasted her, I knew Miss Blue was Nai … and then the butterflies descended on us. I knew then Nai was my fated mate.

I fought it. Fate had to be wrong. Crescent Clan was to blame for my father's death, so how could I love her? If I gave in to my desire for a traitor, it would surely make me weak, too weak to lead. Hadn't Declan threatened exile and disinheritance before? If I accepted Nai as my mate, it'd put my uncle over the edge. I tried to convince myself "Crescent trash" wasn't worth losing everything for…

Ironically, it was my brothers who'd refused to let her go.

Guilt gnawed through my gut for how I'd treated her that whole first semester. Hiding my mate marks, my identity, rejecting her like that. It nearly *killed* me; it definitely drove me to the brink of insanity.

And all the while, I watched in awe at the beauty of her soul. Her kindness, her enthusiasm, her persistence, and her loyalty all proved time and again how she was more than worthy of being my mate. She was my queen.

I dropped my head into my hands and sighed.

'Nai…' I called out through our bond, begging fate to grant me a boon. Instead, sinking dark horror filled me when there was no response. If—no, *when*—we completed our bonding, would I be able to hear her no matter which realm she was in?

Exhaustion burned my eyes and weighed down my limbs, but I wasn't ready to give up. Not yet. I couldn't go to sleep without a scrap of good news. I turned away from the fireplace and returned to the desk.

'Did you find a mage powerful enough to break the protections on that portal?' I asked Justice, slumping into the chair.

His response was immediate. *'No, but I have a lead. Get some sleep. I'm on it.'*

What did I do to deserve such loyal siblings?

'Thank you.'

I set my head on the desk, allowing myself a minute of rest while thinking of Nai's searing blue eyes and how she could look right into my soul. Then the pull of sleep took me.

CHAPTER FIVE

"We have a problem."

Noble's voice pulled me from slumber, and I shot upright. A piece of paper stuck to my face. I batted it away and looked up at my brother wearily. Fatigue, both physical and emotional, clung to me, making my vision blurry. One glance at the dark windows revealed the sun had not yet started to rise.

"What time is it?" I asked, blinking to clear the last vestiges of sleep. "And what do you mean by problem?" I stood and rolled out my neck and shoulders, then took in my brother's serious expression. *Crap.* "You mean there's *another* problem?"

"It's five a.m.," he said, nodding. He grimaced like his next words tasted bad. "Mallory is asking for her father to have a proper alpha burial. Said she can't sleep until she's guaranteed it."

What. The. Mage?

I barked out a laugh.

A proper alpha burial meant he'd be buried in the Garden of Alphas alongside my father and other alphas who'd died after serving their packs for decades. That piece of trash could be buried in the woods, or we could burn him like Declan.

"No way. Proper alpha burials don't go to shady challengers," I growled as I walked to the adjoining bathroom off the study.

Noble grimaced again. "That's what I told her. But she's asking for an exception. Begging, really, saying the high mages spelled her father and tricked him into attacking you. She's saying he was loyal to you."

Tricked? Doubtful. Magically spelled I could buy but with his permission, no doubt. I ran the cold water and cupped my hands, splashing it on my face. As I straightened, Noble set a toothbrush and toothpaste on the ledge.

"Thanks," I told him.

I brushed my teeth, noting the dark circles under my eyes as well as the five o'clock shadow. I looked beyond tired—pathetic, really.

"Any news on Nai?" I asked with a mouthful of toothpaste.

Noble was quiet, but I wasn't sure if he didn't understand my garbled question or if he didn't want to answer. *'Justice? What's the word on that lead?'*

Did my second-in-command even sleep last night? He'd said he had a lead, and then I fell asleep. I should be the one staying up all hours of the night, looking for her.

'Sorry,' Justice said, his words slurred. *'I just nodded off for a second.'*

'That lead?' I prompted, swishing out my mouth.

'Yes, so Surlama's sister, Kalama, is still indentured to the crown, and she has enough power to break those spells.'

And not high enough status to be brought back to High Mage Island with the master teachers for the meeting.

My eyes widened, and I looked at Noble. *'Surlama's sister? Can we even trust her?'*

'Do we have a choice?' Noble and Justice both said in unison.

Touché.

'I've strongly encouraged Kalama to break those spells.' Justice yawned, the long, drawn-out breath echoing through our bond. *'She's working on them now.'*

'Strongly encouraged?' I asked.

'I may have threatened to kill her if she didn't do it,' Justice shot back. *'It was three a.m., and I'm not in the mood for pattycake.'*

I grinned.

'I'm giving you a promotion,' I said just as he strolled into the office.

He looked even worse than I, his black hair messily flattened on one side and sticking up on the other.

"I'm already your second." He yawned again. "You can't promote me any higher than that."

I looked to Noble, who held up his index finger. "Technically, he's right, but … you can make him head of the interrogation team."

I faced Justice with a grin. "Done."

Justice cracked his neck. "Since when do we have an interrogation team?"

"Since now," Noble chuckled.

We all laughed with our normal brotherly banter, and for a brief moment, I *almost* forgot Nai was missing. But with my next breath, the gaping hole in my heart returned. Honor. Nai. They were family, the missing pieces of my heart, and I needed them.

'Nai?' I inhaled and shifted my thinking from my mate to my brother. *'Honor—'*

A loud knock at the door shattered my thoughts, and I groaned.

Please, don't be Mallory.

Noble crossed the room and opened the door.

An ashen-faced guard stumbled in, covered in dried blood. His eyes were wide, and he worked his jaw, but no words came out.

Fur rippled down my arms at the sight of the older shifter, and I looked him over for injuries. "What happened, Simon?"

He was a guard from before my father's time even. He shook his head, and when he spoke, his voice was hoarse. "Kirkland is … gone."

Kirkland and Simon had been in the royal guard together for decades. They were two of the contingency I'd sent with Justice to Dark Row last night, two of the best—because I knew they'd take their responsibilities seriously.

Justice and I exchanged a look, and I could see the guilt in my brother's eyes.

'This isn't your fault,' I told Justice. I knew my brother; he was a protector, sometimes more so than me. These men were probably attacked right after he left, and he'd feel guilt over that.

Justice turned from me to Simon. "Was there an attack?"

It'd take a strong force to bring these two men down.

To my surprise, Simon shook his head.

"I don't really know," he said. "One minute, Kirkland and I were patrolling the east side of Dark Row, talking about the alpha fight, and the next thing ... he was *gone*. There was a rustle of leaves, and I followed after it, but he was pulled away by something so fast my eyes couldn't track it."

I frowned, considering what could take one of my most seasoned guards. "Bear shifter?"

They weren't that fast, but I had no other explanation.

He shook his head and swallowed hard. "No, there are a couple bear shifters helping guard the mages down by Dark Row, so I don't think it's them."

"Bears?" I bristled. "They don't usually help mages."

Shifters tended to stick to their own kind after Declan exiled them all.

Justice nodded, rubbing at his face. "Forgot to tell you last night. The mages pleaded for their help as well, and the bear king sent them."

Bears and wolves working to protect mages at Dark Row? Unheard of…

I shook my head and turned back to Simon. "Tell us what you remember of the attack."

He nodded. "As soon as he was dragged away, I tore off into the woods to find him. Only took a couple seconds to shift, but by the time I got to him … he was dead."

"How long did it take you to find him?" Justice asked.

I knew what he was looking for, and I waited to hear the guard's response. If it took Simon more than a couple of minutes to track someone, then his skills were suffering—either from age or neglect.

"Seconds, sir. Less than a minute after Kirkland disappeared, I found him—or rather his body. But … it didn't look right." Simon blanched, his ashy-gray coloring going even more pale, and he swallowed repeatedly before he managed to speak again. "His body was … husk-like, all around his neck, face, and chest."

The room swam, and my stomach sank as I considered what could cause a death like that.

"A husk?" Noble asked, shooting me a look of horror.

Simon nodded. "Completely ... drained of blood."

What the *hell* did he just say?

"Drained of blood?" Justice parroted.

My brothers both echoed the guard's statements as all three of us reeled with disbelief. Because there was only one thing that could drain blood that fast. Only one species who would—

The guard's lip quivered, and then he started to shake. "His skin was all shriveled..." Simon swallowed, and tears dripped down his weathered cheeks. "Stuck to his bones..." He sniffed. "Like he was *sucked dry*."

Justice and Noble turned to me, their eyes wide.

Shit.

The vampires chose *now* to come down from the cliffs? I sighed. "Thank you, Simon. From now on, we patrol in teams of four. Noble, have Simon checked by a healer and then get an additional dozen guards to Dark Row ASAP."

He nodded, and Noble escorted him to the guard at the door and then returned.

The second the door closed, I turned to my brothers. "We need to make sure our patrols here have sufficient numbers to withstand—"

"You don't really think the rumors about vampire nobility being alive are true, right?" Noble asked.

I closed my eyes and rubbed my temples, wishing there was some way to deny the reality facing us.

Justice cleared his throat. "I heard Uncle Declan speaking once about them. Something about a blood payment."

I jerked my chin up and stared at my brother. "A payment? Of what?"

Because there was only one thing I knew they'd want, and if Declan was paying them in blood...

"Oh, Mother Mage." Noble shook his head. "Don't tell me—"

"Knock-knock." My mother entered the room, holding a tray of food, and we all quieted. As she crossed the room, I noticed her features—even her frame—reflected a strain or tenseness, and I had an epiphany. Whatever horror we'd suffered under Declan, our mother had probably suffered far more. I should have killed him sooner—a lot sooner.

'Don't say anything to worry her,' I said to my brothers. *'She needs time.'*

Probably a lot of it.

Her face brightened when she saw me. "How's my new king? Any word on Nai?"

I shook my head, forcing a smile even as my heart sank. "Still working on it. I did get a message to her, I think, and Justice has a mage trying to break the protection spell on the portal."

She nodded, setting down the tray. My brothers and I dug into the honey-baked ham, scrambled eggs, bacon, and hash browns that were piled high on the platter but diminishing quickly.

My mom gave me a tremulous smile. "Honey, while you're here, I need to talk to you about the main kitchen remodel."

My shoulders tightened with fresh, *additional* tension. "Kitchen remodel?"

She nodded. "Chuck has been asking for a remodel budget for a decade now, and I think—"

"Give me a list of what you and Chuck want as well as pricing, and we'll get it done," Noble said. "Rage has enough on his plate without having to worry about a kitchen remodel."

'Thanks.' I shot my brother a smile filled with relief and gratitude. *'That would've been the straw that broke my camel's back.'*

Mom smiled. "Will do, dear."

After giving us all a kiss on the cheek, she left, and I felt both worse and better because she seemed to stand a little taller.

Was this really what my uncle had done all day? Because it was a lot harder than I thought it'd be. I was constantly putting out fires with barely any time to think about Nai or myself.

"I'll handle the kitchen remodel," Noble told me. "But I'd also like to hire an assistant."

I nodded. "Done. Approved. Whatever you need."

Justice and I met each other's gazes.

"I need you to tell me everything you know about the vampire situation, preferably *before* we get to Dark Row to check out where Kirkland was killed."

Justice nodded. "We can talk on our way over. First, let's go check in with Kalama."

We all stood, and I looked from Justice to Noble and back. "If *anyone* hears *anything* about Nai—"

"We'll let you know," they both said in unison.

If Nai wasn't in my bed tonight, I'd burn the entire realm down tomorrow.

CHAPTER SIX

We stepped into the library, and my gut churned. Acrid smoke filled the air. Justice and I wound our way through the aisles to the back of the room. Alpha Academy classes were paused until the master mages returned. Shifting over to a new king was a process, but we'd be back up and running in no time. And I'd have Nai by my side.

Kalama stood in front of the onyx door, wearing a grease-stained apron over a fitted t-shirt and pants. The kitchen maid and sister of Surlama glared at the entrance to High Mage Island as if her fierce expression alone could make it pop open.

On either side of the door sat a shallow metal bowl, each of them filled with smoking herbs.

"How are things going?" I asked.

Kalama wheeled on me. "If things were going well, I'd have the damn door open."

Okay. She obviously took after her sister in the personality department.

"So ... not well," Justice said.

"There are fifteen spells on this door, Prince. It's not quite as easy as making pie in the kitchen."

"Do you need anything from me?" I asked.

She grinned like a cat who'd just spotted prey. "Well, actually, I was telling Justice—"

Justice cleared his throat. "Is there anything that *I* might be able to do to help you get through the protection enchantments *faster*?"

I frowned; my brother was clearly hiding something from me.

She barked a hard laugh and then shook her head. "You can't help me, *Second.*"

She spat his pack rank out like it was acid, and I caught a glimpse of what was going on. Maybe.

"You must not be a powerful enough witch, then," Justice taunted, his expression hardening.

'Justice, what does she need?' I asked.

He shook his head. *'I don't trust her with what she claims she needs. Remember who her sister is.'*

"Listen, Midnight Heir. I said *you* can't help me." Then her gaze flicked to me. "But *you* can."

Pursing my lips, I shook my head. I knew where this was going. But, with any luck, I'd be wrong. "What do you want?" I growled.

She raised a well-manicured eyebrow. "Alpha blood would increase my odds of getting this open faster."

Of course. Just like her sister, they always wanted blood.

"No," Justice snarled and bared his teeth.

'Brother, if she needs it—'

'Look what happened with her sister. They cannot be trusted with blood.' Justice glared at her.

It was my brother's job to protect me, so I wasn't going to begrudge him for doing this, but if this would help her…

"I give you my blood, you'll release the protection spells?"

Justice groaned.

She nodded, her long tight braids slithering up and down her shoulders.

"But I'll also need you to temporarily release me from my servitude bond," she said. "It suppresses my magic here on the island."

I sighed.

Well, I didn't need or even want her around anyway. She was a liability. I could get a new kitchen maid with half the baggage, so I'd give her a better offer.

"If you can get those spells off, I'll release you *permanently*. But without you being bonded, what's going to keep you from walking out that door?"

"Her integrity?" Justice snickered, and I had to take a deep breath to keep from cracking a smile.

I nudged him. *'Not sure insulting her will help.'*

"Fine," she said, her lips pulling up on one side to

give Justice a cruel half-smile. "I'll bind myself *here,* to the library, first."

She pulled a small dagger from around her waist and pricked her finger. Then she dripped a single drop into the smoking herbs. "I, Kalama, *willingly* bind my body and soul to Alpha Academy's library until I break the protection spells on the portal to High Mage Island."

The air crackled with magic, and Kalama shuddered once before she looked at me expectantly.

I glanced at Justice.

'Don't look at me, bro. I'm not king. I can't let her go.'

Ugh.

"Fine. What do I need to do?" Following her instructions, I slid my own dagger from its sheath at my waist and then pricked my middle finger.

'For the record, I think giving your blood to this woman is a horrible idea,' Justice said as I allowed one drop to land in each bowl.

'Noted,' I said.

Taking in a deep breath, I did something I really hoped wouldn't come back to bite me in the butt. "I, Courage Midnight, Alpha King, hereby release Kalama from her servant bondage so that she'll be able to destroy *all* the spells, enchantments, hexes, and curses on the portal separating Alpha Island from High Mage Island. Once *all* the protection spells, enchantments, hexes, and curses are eliminated, she'll be released from her bond of servitude here on Alpha Island."

Kalama's expression hardened. "That's a bit more than necessary."

I shrugged. "I've learned word choice matters quite a bit when it comes to magical oaths."

She yanked the bowls containing my blood away from me and then spun on her heel, waving us off. "Now, let me work. I'll let you know when it's done."

Justice and I left and then made our way down to the docks.

'I gotta say, watching you prick your finger like that gives me the willies,' Justice said as he started the boat.

'There's nothing I won't do to bring Nai home,' I told him. Didn't he understand? She was my other half. My brother needed to fall in love so he'd know what this all-consuming feeling was like.

I considered Kalama's dark magic, so much like her sister's—and then my thoughts went back to the vampire issue I needed to deal with. The idea that they *drank* blood and that my uncle seemed to have allowed them to … I dunno … hunt? It gave me the shivers and made me angry at the same time.

My disgust, both with the practice as well as my uncle's apparent willingness to go along with it, hadn't lessened. How many deaths had occurred due to vampires draining people while we'd been lied to about it? How many vampires were there left? I had way too many questions and needed more answers.

"Let's go to Dark Row. I want to sniff around the place Kirkland died," I told Justice.

He nodded, and we sped across the water in a speedboat toward Dark Row where I hoped to get additional information that would allow for something other than a *blood payment* to the freaking vampires.

The last war between the magical races was hundreds of years ago. The vampires were all but wiped out, causing what small numbers they had to retreat to caves to survive. How long did vampires live? Unless they had continued to breed … the thought made me shiver. Could they breed?

I pulled down my sunglasses and rubbed my eyes as Justice slowed the boat and brought it alongside the dock.

"Do you want to see Kirkland's body first or talk with the mages?" Justice asked.

A shriveled corpse? I grunted and jumped out to tie the boat off. "Let's chat up the mages. I can imagine what Kirkland's body will look like, and I can wait to see that."

Justice raised his eyebrows and then clapped me on the back as he stepped off the boat.

"You getting squeamish?" he asked, shaking his head. "Don't tell me the rumors are true."

I finished with the last buoy and straightened with a groan. "What rumors?"

Because if I had to deal with one more thing…

"Nai has turned you soft," Justice said.

I shook my head at his antics. Then, together, we strolled toward the remains of Dark Row.

At the southernmost edge, two colorful tents stood huddled together. The yellow and green silk was streaked with soot and ash, but I couldn't tell if these tents were survivors of the fire or new installations.

The scorched earth near where Surlama's tent had once been remained empty as did the area surrounding it.

I raised one eyebrow at my brother. *'You totally burned down Dark Row.'* My voice was light, but he winced.

'It was an accident ... sort of.'

Four Midnight guards dressed in black leather armor stood at the edge of the blackened earth, and twenty yards south of them was a large bear shifter. It was crazy to see bears working alongside us to help the mages. It was… something I never thought possible but always wanted, for all shifters to work together again.

Guilt wiggled through me at the sight of the bear, leftover shame from Nanny Bess, and without saying a word, Justice and I detoured toward our men.

"King Courage," said Richie, the eldest of the guards, and all four of them straightened.

I gave Richie a tight smile. "It doesn't seem like they're making much progress." I waved to the expanse of ruin. "Or are they not going to rebuild it all?"

Richie shrugged, but his eyes darted a quick glance to the cluster of tents. "The word is the lower mages have lost half a dozen men in the last few days. Whatever is hunting them has been picking them off, one by one. I think they're all staying south for that reason."

More evidence against the vampires as they were allegedly banished to the northern cliffs.

"Right," I muttered, then jerked my head toward the group of mages. "Let's see if we can get some more info from them today."

As luck would have it, the young brunette woman, who I'd originally met at the alpha castle, sat on a small wooden stool at the outskirt of the tents. She was grinding spices with a mortar and pestle, her head bowed over her work. She muttered indistinctly to herself, not even noticing our approach.

"Excuse me," I said and was rewarded with a sharp gasp and a glare from the female mage.

"What do you want?" she snapped, pausing with the pestle in hand. "Come to gloat over our losses? Or are you going to pull your guards again?"

What was with these people? They hated me, the high mages, and pretty much everyone, it seemed.

"Why would you say that?" Justice shot back. "He sent guards—"

"Not enough!" she spat back. "Not until one of his own was killed, and even now, they all stay in their little groups, doing nothing to help."

I raised my chin and glanced over my shoulder. "Richie!"

The four guards approached.

"Where are the other five sets of men?" I asked. As

soon as he started to list the various locations, I shook my head and cut him off. "Pull them all into Dark Row. The goal is to help these people recoup, not to patrol *all* of Mageville." I raised my eyebrows at the female mage. "Right?"

She winced. "If you pull them all in, then the townspeople will be left unprotected."

I shook my head. "There are thousands of mages here. If you don't have your own force, I suggest you create one. *This isn't my problem.*"

"We're not allowed to, *bone*head." She glared at me. "That's why we came to you in the first place. The high mages don't allow the mages any type of military force or mage collective."

'Did she really just call me a bonehead?' I asked Justice.

He snorted but kept his attention on the mage.

Apparently, the high mages were control freaks, and the shifters were left protecting their people. That wasn't right. Why not let them make their own police force?

It dawned on me then.

The mages would become more powerful that way. The lower-level mages outnumbered the advanced, master, and high mages, ten to one. If they were allowed to train together and create some type of organized force…

I shook my head. Another problem for future-Rage to deal with.

"We're here trying to help. I suggest you stop calling

the alpha king names," Justice growled, and she dropped her chin to her chest. Justice ignored her obvious embarrassment and plowed on. "And maybe do what you can to help us understand what the hell is going on." He crossed his arms over his chest. "Unless you'd rather us just leave."

The girl's skin turned a healthy shade of pink. She swallowed hard before she looked up at us—this time with tears in her eyes. "What do you want to know?"

"Are the vampires the ones attacking your people? Are they all drained of blood?"

She frowned, eyes widening in alarm. "Vampires?"

I felt like I was having a conversation with a two-year-old, in a foreign language.

"Vampires. Blood-sucking creatures—"

"You mean the blood-mages?" she asked and then nodded. "Yes. They're coming down from the cliffs to feed," she muttered, almost to herself. "Plus, taking blood for their spells..."

Whoa. Whoa. "What?" My eyes widened. "Feed? You've known about them this whole time?"

She flicked me an irritated gaze, "Everyone knows. But your uncle and Surlama kept them satiated. Now, they're just ... running amok."

My head spun with her words. My uncle ... and *Surlama*?

"Surlama?" I interrupted her, my eyes widening in horror as I thought of how the witch had always demanded blood from Nai—and me.

She wouldn't have been … a … blood mage, would she?

If the vampires were really blood-mages … and used blood in spells as well as consumed it, then…

The woman looked up at me with a sugary smile. "Surlama was a blood mage. But if you want to call them vampires, they don't care." She cocked her head to the side. "Didn't you know?"

That meant that…

"Kalama!" Justice and I both said at the same time.

'Noble?'

'What's up?'

I nearly sagged with relief at his voice. *'I need you to go check on Kalama in the library. Take a few guards with you, and...'*

'And what?' Noble asked when I grew silent.

After all this, I couldn't very well let her get away.

'And detain her. I'll need to talk to her when I get back.'

I turned my attention back to the female mage. It was time to divide and conquer, and right now, I trusted my brother's head better than mine. "Tell my brother everything you know about blood-mages." I pointed to my brother. "He'll stay here with you."

'Sorry, bro,' I told Justice.

He shrugged. *'I understand.'*

"Richie…" I turned to the guard. "I need you to go through Mageville and pick two dozen young mage men who have some semblance of wit about them. Teach them how to run patrols, defense, craft weapons, anything so they can learn to take care of themselves." I wasn't the damn alpha of mages. They needed to figure their own crap out.

I spotted another group of four guards and called them over. "I need you four to come with me. We need to go examine where Kirkland was attacked."

'I'll meet you at the boat in an hour,' I told Justice.

As I strode away, I let my wolf surge to the surface. Dropping to all fours, I raced past Dark Row and headed north.

So many thoughts swirled around in my head. Where in the mage hell was Nai? What would I do if the vampires really were back? How deep and dark did my uncle's secrets go? Could I even do this alone? Surlama had been one of them the entire time! There was a reason we used to be Shifter Island. There was a reason we all banded together. Because when enemies like *blood mages* came calling, we stood stronger *together.* Something I thought we'd been doing just as wolves. But if my uncle had simply been paying the vampires off with a blood payment, then … well, that didn't sit well with me. I wouldn't do that.

My paws pounded the ground, and my men ran behind me as I followed the sickly smell of death and dark magic.

'Any word on Nai?' I asked Noble.

'No, brother, I'm sorry. After we detain Kalama, I'll go to the mortal portal and see if her aunt is working again. I'll try to pry some more information.'

A small measure of relief wormed through me. At least, we were doing something.

I tracked the scent of decay, blood, and rotten flesh to the base of the north cliffs above Dark Row and pulled to a stop as the scent became overwhelming. I lifted my snout from the ground to lessen the smell as I slipped into the thick tree line. The underbrush was smashed and broken, and there were clear tracks where a body had been dragged. My heart squeezed with guilt, but my nostrils flared in anger. I *hated* that one of my own went out like this.

When I reached the base of a large oak, I saw Kirkland, or rather what was left of him. His entire form was a shriveled husk, lying in a collapsed guard uniform; his skin was mottled and putrid.

I wrinkled my nose at the stench.

Blood magic. Death. Wolf. And another smell ... like carrion times a million.

How had it taken only *seconds* for the blood mage to do that?

I tipped my head back and howled long and deep. I was angry. Beyond angry. My uncle left me a legit shit storm as an inheritance. And totally unprepared. Worse than that was the sinking feeling of despair hanging in my chest. I wanted my fated mate with me, by my side to help me figure this mess out. Regardless of what Justice said, Nai didn't make me weaker; she made me stronger.

There was something I'd intended to do the first

day as king, but I'd put it off because I wanted her with me for this historic moment. However, I couldn't wait any longer. Now that the blood mages, aka vampires, were back, I needed to unite our people before we were picked off and washed out.

Turning, I spun and headed for the dock.

'Justice? You ready?'

'I'm on my way to the dock now.'

I pushed harder into the run with my guards following behind me.

'Noble,' I said, scouting the area with the other wolves as we ran back to Dark Row. *'Prepare to send out thousands of invitations.'*

My brother's energy bristled before he responded. *'Invitations for what?'*

I sent out my next thought to both Noble and Justice. *'I'll officially declare the island to be Shifter Island once again. Every single shifter animal needs to come home.'*

I felt the rightness at my decision echoed in my siblings' thoughts.

'We'll be reunited as shifters again,' I declared.

Then I sent my thoughts out to the other wolves. *'Go get Kirkland's body and bring it home so we can give him a proper burial.'* They nodded, and I met each set of eyes. *'Be careful. The vampires are back, and they've left the cliffs to hunt. Stay together.'*

'Yes, Alpha,' they responded in unison, but one of them whined.

'What?' I demanded.

'Keep alpha safe.'

I considered his foresight for only a heartbeat. The reality was that as soon as they shifted into their human form, they'd be at risk. *'No. I'll run to the boat and be fine. You need to stay together.'*

I waited until all four wolves took off. Then, I ran toward the dock.

'Rage?' Noble spoke through our bond, and his voice sounded weary. *'I'm... I have some bad news.'*

More bad news?

'What is it now?' I asked, racing through the wilderness of Mageville. My thoughts jumped ahead to the other task I'd asked Noble to do, and I tacked on an additional question. *'And did you get Kalama detained? I—'*

'That's just it,' he replied. *'She's gone.'*

Shock punched me in the gut, and I stumbled on my run through the burnt remnants of Dark Row. *'What do you mean, she's gone?'*

I regained my footing and picked up my pace, full-on sprinting in my hurry to get back to the boat and Shifter Island.

'Is the portal door open?' I asked. *'Can you get into High Mage Island?'*

I wrestled with the barrage of thoughts: how was I supposed to go get Nai back, draft the invitations and send those out, not to mention the logistics of where to put everyone...?

No ... everything else would wait for Nai. She

would always be my top priority.

'The door is closed, bro. There's no handle or knob... and I can't push it open. But it no longer shocks when I touch it.'

Mother effin' Mage!

Did she somehow find a way around my words? I remembered my oath and snarled. She'd taken off the protection spell but didn't open the damn door!

'Send out as many guards as we can spare to look for Kalama,' I snapped. *'I want her—'*

'I'm already on it,' Noble said with a sigh. *'I'm sorry.'*

Fuming, I nevertheless shot back the truth. *'It's not your fault.'*

It was mine. And Kalama's.

I growled as I burst through the trees. Just south of the dock, I shifted into my human form with a bellow of frustration.

Justice ran toward me, slowing his pace as I strode forward, cursing with every step.

My blood boiled, and I met Justice's worried gaze and snarled. "That witch!"

How could I have trusted her? I went over my oath, wondering how I'd screwed up with my wording. She shouldn't have been able to leave without removing all the damn wards.

"What's wrong?" Justice asked, matching my rapid stride, step for step.

I shook my head, grinding my teeth together to keep from vomiting vitriolic wrath onto my brothers. None of this was their fault.

My pulse roared in my ears; every beat of my heart was fuel for my fury. Fur bristled along my skin, and I struggled to hold on to my form. There was nothing my wolf could do right now anyway.

Sucking in one deep breath after another, I said nothing until we were both in the boat and away from shore.

"She's gone," I said, glaring at our island.

Justice cocked his head to the side, and his worried expression spoke volumes. "Kalama?"

I nodded, but even then, my thoughts went to Nai. She was gone, too.

"Then, the wards are gone, right?" he asked.

I told him what Noble had said and then asked him what he'd learned from the female mage.

"Are you sure you want to hear it right now?" Justice asked.

Glaring at him, I crossed my arms over my chest. "Somehow, I don't think there's going to be a better time than now."

He gave me the rundown as we crossed the waters: blood mages were just as powerful as the high mages, except they were the masters of blood magic—aka *dark* magic—which was why Dark Row was called *Dark* Row.

Most of the blood mages had been killed during the war hundreds of years ago, but the High Mage Council had left a few females alive, Surlama and Kalama being two of them. When Kalama was caught hunting on

Alpha Island, Declan, with help from at least one of the high mages, bound her magic and forced her into servitude, something my uncle was *apparently* quite fond of doing.

Blood mages could boost their magic by consuming blood as well as using magical blood in their spells.

"So all that blood Surlama took … was she able to do all the stuff Nai can?" I swallowed. "I mean if Surlama drank her blood?"

The idea made my stomach churn.

"From what Liv said, no." Justice took a deep breath. "She said Surlama could increase her own power by drinking Nai's blood because Nai is so powerful. Or, the witch could use it for blood magic—like the healing elixir."

"I'm not even sure what to do with that information right now." I rubbed my temples as a dull ache spread through my head. "Speaking of healing elixir, I hope there's some in the infirmary."

Justice clapped me on the back and then throttled back the motor as we approached the island.

"Are we going to the library first?" he asked.

I nodded. "I have to try the door one more time."

For the first time, I started to doubt. Would we get Nai back?

CHAPTER SEVEN

UNFORTUNATELY, Noble was right. No matter how much pushing or prying we did, the black onyx door remained closed. While I could now touch the smooth black stone without being electrocuted, I remained powerless to open it.

An hour later, as the afternoon pressed on, I stepped into Declan's office and pulled to a stop. Behind me, Justice bumped into me with a grunt.

"What the—oh, my Mother Mage," he muttered, echoing my awe.

The smell of fresh paint hung heavy in the air.

The walls were no longer yellow but a soft gray. The stone floor was covered with a thick, plush area rug with the same gray in a pattern with taupe and blues. All the furniture had been replaced. The desk was a sleek minimalist style made of gray wood, and the chair behind the desk was one of those expensive ergonomic chairs, in the same dusty ash color as the wood of the desk. Opposite the desk sat a long couch upholstered in charcoal velvet, and to the right of the couch were two chairs separated by a chest-style end table.

Modern masculine art in splashes of blues and grays decorated two of the walls, and as I moved into the room, I smiled at the personal touches: pictures of me and my brothers throughout the years as well as several with my mom. A picture from our parents' wedding...

I stepped past a coffee table; the natural stain on the irregularly shaped wood added a warm, rustic touch to the ambiance.

"You didn't give me enough time to finish," Noble said with a huff, but one glance told me he was pleased.

"This is ... *perfect*," I said, grinning. Gone were the memories and remnants of my uncle's ghost and the darkness from our childhood.

As I stepped around my desk, my gaze dropped to the pictures there, and the grin slid from my face.

There, in the right corner, was a picture of Nai dressed as Miss Blue. Her eyes were wide as she looked innocently at the camera. I had no idea who had taken this photo or how Noble got it, but ... I loved it. With a sigh, I remembered the moment I'd kissed her and realized she was my fated mate.

There was another photo of Nai with Noble, both of them in the cafeteria, my mate wearing a hairnet over her white, platinum-blond hair. And then another one of the two of us standing in the middle of the field in Montana, me holding her tightly, right after the fight with Declan. I had my eyes closed and my chin resting on her head, her silvery hair billowing in the freezing wind.

I looked up at my brother with surprise. "Were you paparazzi-stalking me and Nai?"

Noble snickered, and Justice joined in.

"I just figured, one day, you'd be happy for some memories," Noble said.

I nodded and slid into the chair. "Thanks, bro."

Not even a full breath later, our mom stepped into the room.

"I thought I heard you boys," she said, her eyes widening as she took in the new digs. "Noble Midnight," she breathed, "I *love* it." Her gaze fell on me, and she tsked. "You haven't eaten! I'll be right back with lunch."

That was Mom; she showed her love with food and hugs. I had no complaints.

While we ate, we discussed the invitation to the other shifters, logistics, and such. The entire time Noble jotted down notes.

An hour later, Noble thrust a thick decree in my face, neatly typed on a scroll with a wax seal and all.

"This will make it official," he said. "You sign this, and every single shifter species can live on the island. You'll only preside over the wolves, so no dictatorship, which means you'll have to work with the leaders of each shifter race on a quorum."

I sighed, nodding. Did I like having final say? Yes. Was it right? Not for the other species. "Do we have enough room? Did you draw up fair boundaries and still give us our own territories?"

Noble winced. "It will be tight, depending on how many say yes and how prolifically they've reproduced, but yes, the decree states a clear border around the school, castle, and four clan lands."

I sank in relief. At least, I wouldn't have to ask *my* people to give up any of their original lands. Anything the wolves took after Declan booted the other shifters would be returned, but we got to keep our territory. Thank the Mother Mage for old land maps.

Reaching out, I picked up the pen and then glanced at each of my brothers.

This was a huge moment for me, for us. Nai and Honor *should* be here.

Now, with Kalama missing, I had no way to get Nai back. The thought made the pit in my stomach open wider.

Gripping the pen, I signed my name in large, cursive scroll.

King Courage Midnight.

I stared at my signature as emotions rolled through me. *This* would be my legacy.

My uncle had torn the shifter races apart. I would unite us again.

Mother Mage willing.

"Send out the invitations. Give the leader of each shifter race a copy of the royal decree as well as the alpha of each wolf pack. Post a copy on the castle wall and another in the academy. I want to make sure our people understand what's going on and have ample notice."

Noble nodded as Justice placed a hand on my shoulder. "Father would be proud."

Emotion clogged my throat, but my thoughts jumped to Nai. Even more than my father, I wanted my mate. I wanted to hear Nai's excitement. Her pride in my plan.

Noble stepped in front of me. "What should I tell the shifters who voice complaints about the new decree? Shall we offer a Q and A tomorrow night? Then, you can answer questions and concerns?"

That sounded awful.

My gaze flicked to Justice, who shook his head. *'If you allow them to start, the complaints will never end.'*

I grinned as he stated my thoughts.

"Tell them to shove it," I replied to Noble. "This new law is a long time coming, but it isn't up for discussion. There's nothing they can do about it."

Noble nodded and then left the room, leaving Justice and me alone.

I dropped my face into my hands. "What a nightmare of a day. I can't believe Surlama and her twin were blood mages this entire time."

Justice grunted. "I suspect we don't even know all of it … but I trust Liv. She had no reason to lie. Plus, it makes sense why Surlama hoarded all that blood."

I shivered. Why hadn't I questioned the mass amounts of blood that woman needed?

"Do you think Kalama's the last one left? Or are the others still in the cliffs?" Justice asked.

I recoiled at the thought and then raised my chin to look at my brother. "There could be more. Didn't Liv say there were? Or maybe I made that up. I don't remember. But I do know Kalama couldn't have left the island when Kirkland was killed on Dark Row, so…" I cleared my throat.

Justice finished my thought: "There must be more."

I shook my head. "I have no idea what Declan was doing or what kinds of deals he had going on. I knew he was shady, but this … this is *unforgivable*."

Justice nodded. "Like how many of our people did he allow to be drained as a blood payment and then lie to us that they'd died under different circumstances?"

I growled and then shoved away the thought before it could enrage me.

My gaze landed on the new clock, and I started at the time. How was it late afternoon already? Yesterday I'd said if Nai wasn't back by morning, I was going to raise hell.

I sat back in my chair and closed my eyes, debating my options. I *wanted* to believe something was keeping her from me and her grandfather would make sure she was safe. I had to believe it because that was my only hope.

"Tomorrow," I breathed. "One more day, and if Nai isn't here, I'm calling a meeting with the High Mage Council, consequences be damned."

Justice nodded. "I think that's fair."

"What if they don't come?" I asked, sitting up suddenly. "What if the shifters like being away? I don't think we can take on vampires or blood mages and whatever other threats may come our way. Like, what if the mages—"

"Selkies will come," Justice said. "Bears may not, considering. Foxes will come, and I suspect the hawks and falcons will too. They've long made their desire to return home a public affair."

"Panthers probably won't," I offered. "Uncle Declan betrayed them even worse than the bears." The memory of my mother telling us about Declan killing the panther king *in front of his own children* still made me sick. All because he wouldn't vacate the island. That story had made me fear Declan even more. Only now did I understand why she'd told us so many awful things about him; she was doing all she could so we wouldn't become like him. Somehow, I'd missed that message for a while … until Nai. She'd helped me see the truth.

'Nai...' I called, wanting but no longer hopeful.

But even though I didn't expect a response, the silence still hurt.

The rest of the day passed quickly. By evening, we'd received word from the selkie king, fox queen, and tiger queen, graciously accepting the invitation to return. Over the coming weeks, they'd return to Shifter Island. The fox and lion queens asked for supplies to help rebuild their communities as well as boats and some crap that I wasn't even sure whether we had.

Noble, with administrative prowess, handled all of the logistics.

As for the bear, panther, and hawk leaders ... we'd yet to hear from the bear king or panther queen, but the hawks said they needed more time to think about it.

Finally, my head and body couldn't handle any more. After a long shower, I lay down in my bed ... for the first time since I was king. I'd been hesitant to change quarters just in case Nai came looking for me, but Justice put a note on my old Midnight dorm door and sent me to my new rooms in the castle, just off of the main dining hall. These had been guest quarters before, so they held no bad memories for me.

Of course, as soon as the lights were off, my mind started to spin. I sighed, stroking the black satin sheets as I wished for sleep and ran through various to-dos in my head. I needed to get the other kings and queens up to speed on the situation concerning the blood mages, aka vampires. More shifters here would allow for turns patrolling the island and Dark Row. Trust would take time, and working together again would probably have some hiccups, but I'd do whatever was necessary. We were stronger together. My father believed that, and so did I.

As for Nai…?

Anger and hurt coursed through me when I thought about her.

I almost hoped she was kidnapped because the idea that she might have left willingly hurt more.

Eventually, the exhaustion of the past few days caught up. Like a hundred-pound boulder tied to my consciousness, I sank deeply into the abyss of nothingness.

CHAPTER EIGHT

THE CREAKING of my bedroom door yanked me awake. Still sluggish with fatigue, I glanced to the clock to see I'd only been asleep twenty minutes.

Noble better have a damn good reason…

"Someone better be dead," I growled as I sat up, looking to the doorway … and my heart stopped beating in my chest—

"Nai?" I gasped, recognizing her backlit silhouette.

At the same time, my mate cried, "Rage!"

Her voice shook me to my core.

I moved so fast that I had no memory of even shifting my weight. One moment, I was in bed, and then next, I stood before her, scanning her for injuries, rope burns, any signs of torture.

And, Mother Mage … she had plenty.

Her beautiful face was marred with dirt and scratches that were not quite healed, and her eyes were puffy like she'd been crying—a lot. There were blood and soot under her nails, and her shirt was torn.

"What … who hurt you?" I gathered her into my arms and pressed her to my chest, relieved when she melted into me without protest. "Was this your grandfather's doing?" I growled with the thought as I rubbed one hand up and down her back, pressing her body into mine. "If so, I'll kill him."

She pulled away just enough to rise up on her toes and kiss my neck. The feel of her body pressing into mine caused me to loosen my hold, and then she took my face in her hands.

"Oh, Rage," she whispered, her voice breaking. Her expression crumpled, and fresh tears glimmered in her eyes. "He's … dying." Tears spilled down her cheeks, and she buried her face in my chest.

I held her, letting her grief pour out in racking sobs and disjointed sentences, trying to understand what she meant. After a hard shudder, she sucked in a deep breath, sniffed, and then pulled herself together, at least enough to speak.

"It's bad," she said, wiping the moisture from her face. "I went to help grandpa at your coronation. He told me he needed to formally declare me as his heir before he died. I thought I'd sneak right back after we signed the heir declaration, but then I got thrust into an initiation obstacle course to prove myself worthy." She blinked, offering me a watery smile. "I thought we'd be able to still speak through the bond. I'm *so* sorry, Rage. I'm so *freaking* sorry." Her voice broke.

Her grandfather was dying? At least, her aunt was right about that. But she left ... willingly.

"Heir declaration? Obstacle course?" What the hell was she talking about?

She exhaled, long and slow, then shook her head. Her gaze dropped, and she brushed her fingers over my lips. "I-I don't want to talk about that place right now. Can we put that all on hold, please?" She took another breath. "I really want to talk about ... *us*."

As she spoke that last word, her fingers trailed down my neck and then my chest, leaving a trail of fire in their wake.

I forced a swallow and dug my fingers into her hips, my entire body trembling. I couldn't hold it in any longer. I couldn't keep my shit together. "I ... I thought you were *kidnapped,* Nai. You ... you left me. On my coronation day." I swallowed hard again. "You did that *willingly?*"

I needed something more than an apology—I needed some way to make sense of...

"That *hurt*."

A tear slid down her cheek.

It was like a dam had burst, and I couldn't stop. "Why did it have to be right then? Why couldn't you tell me? Why ... you left without even a thought," I growled.

Fresh tears trickled down her face, and she nodded.

"I-I was scared you wouldn't let me go," she whispered. "My grandfather said we had a limited amount of time to record my name in the books—and I had to be there for it. He said if I don't inherit his spirit magic, the one that lets him raise the dead, like Honor, it will go to Kian and the other high mage councilmen."

The breath whooshed out of me as I thought of creepy-ass Kian having more power. "Yeah, we can't let that happen…"

That would be worse than Declan 2.0. Way worse.

She sighed and ran her hand through her silky hair; black soot fell all around her. "I came back as soon as I could. I've barely slept since I left." She punctuated her statement with a yawn. "Not that it looks like you've slept much, either." She stared into my eyes, and more tears oozed from the corners of her eyes. "I was so worried you'd think I just left you."

I reached up and brushed away her tears with the pad of my thumbs. "Dammit, woman." I rested my forehead to hers and whispered the bitter truth. "You nearly broke me."

Nai lifted her chin. "I'm sorry," she said, her voice breathy. "I love you, Rage. I love you so much."

My lips parted as the air in the room charged with energy. Need coursed through me as my heart thundered wildly against my ribs.

"Nai." I spoke her name—both a plea and a blessing—and I let my fingers dance over her satin skin, down her neck until my palm rested against her chest. Her heart thumped against my hand, and her breath quickened. Leaning forward, she sucked my bottom lip into her mouth, and I groaned, every single muscle in my body clenching with need.

"Rage…" she panted against my lips.

I walked her backward, closing the door as I boxed her in. Pressing my body to hers, I trailed kisses down her skin and then slowly dragged the tip of my tongue up her neck. She arched to give me better access as I scented her, and I slipped my hand under her shirt to caress her breast. "I love you, Nai," I growled with a squeeze, and then I nipped at the sensitive spot just below her ear. "You are mine, *mate*."

She moaned, melting into me as she raked her fingers down my back. "Yes," she breathed and then slid her tongue into my mouth.

Our tongues tangled, stroking against one another while stoking the passion between us.

"We have to seal our bond," she said.

I gripped her hips, grinding against her. *Yes.*

"Please?" she begged, writhing against me as she fumbled with my boxers.

Oh … hell yes.

I scooped my hands under her thighs and lifted Nai up, cupping her butt. Her body was soft where mine was hard, and I wanted nothing more than to be drunk on Nai.

We tumbled back onto the bed, and our kisses grew frantic. Nai's shirt disappeared as did her pants. I stared down at her, her pale skin a stark contrast to the black silk sheets. Three articles of clothing were all that stood between us now—and we had all night to explore one another.

I lowered myself onto her, bracing my weight on my elbows, and then kissed her slowly.

"We need to seal it before they break it," she breathed, again tugging on the waistband of my underwear.

Her words doused my passion, and I yanked back, my brow furrowed with confusion. "What?" I asked.

Her eyes were wide and frantic. She didn't look lost in a haze of lust ... she looked *scared*.

"What did you just say?" I repeated.

Her lower lip trembled. "The high mages heard how you called all of the shifters back to the island. They know you'll be a strong leader, and some of them are worried you'll be *too* strong. A threat."

"Too strong?" I sat back on the bed and stared at her. "Too strong for what?"

She swallowed, her chest still heaving with each breath, but her fear was palpable. "They want total control. I think they had it with Declan—I'm sure they did—but you aren't doing anything the way they think you should."

"That's their problem," I snapped, irritated that the High Mage Council believed they should have any say in what happens on Shifter Island.

"Yes, but they said if I'm going to be going to school

there, we can't be bonded mates. That I'll spy for you. I overheard them talking. If they break our mate bond before we seal it … it will be broken forever."

I blinked, stunned as I finally understood her fear. I also processed her words about going to school there.

Over my dead body.

How dare they!

Those evil asshats.

A full-on howl ripped from my throat, and Nai scooted backward as my wolf rushed to the surface. My arms broke out into pelts of black fur, and I struggled to rein in my wolf.

Nai dropped her chin to her chest, her expression crumpled in defeat.

I looked my mate up and down and growled, forcing myself to stay human. "Oh, I will have you, Nai Crescent. All of you. But not because of their threat to our bond. They will not force this moment."

She looked up at me with a sad smile. "If I go back and we're not mated, then they may get their wish and break our bond forever."

Unbridled rage coursed through my entire being. "Let. Them. *Try.*" Fire danced over my skin as my magic flared out of control with my emotions. "I'm the alpha king, and you are my fated mate. If they come between us, I'll dismantle them, limb by limb, and use them for firewood before I burn their entire realm to the ground."

She inched forward on her knees and then stroked

my cheek. "Please, Rage? I can't handle a world in which we aren't mated."

Her pain and fear pummeled my pride. I nodded, understanding her emotions, and yet I would not be their pawn. "Me neither."

I stared at Nai, my heart aching for her. This wasn't a time for rash decisions, nor was it a time for foolish stubbornness. If I defied Nai *now*, that would only play into their hands. No, my mate was more important to me than anything … anyone … or any*time*. I wouldn't let her go back unmated.

"Holy Mother Mage, Nai. You are irresistible…"

I took a deep breath and gently lay her down.

Tomorrow, I'd draw up a thousand different war plans for every possible situation the high mages could throw at us.

But *tonight*…

I'd make Nai mine.

And I'd become hers.

Forever.

Buy Midnight Truth, Book Four here.

USA TODAY BESTSELLING AUTHORS
LEIA STONE
RAYE WAGNER
SHIFTER
ISLAND
BOOK 4: MIDNIGHT TRUTH

READ MORE FROM THE AUTHORS

You can read more of Leia Stone's books here.

You can read more of Raye Wagner's books here.

Printed in Great Britain
by Amazon